The House That Dwells...

This house lives in a world of its own.
Those who enter it may never leave it.
Those who leave it will never forget it.

Fright House

House

L. Roberson

FRIGHT HOUSE

BY L. ROBERSON

Cover Artwork
By Chris Cartwright
http://www.digitelldesign.com

CONTENTS

For
Karon, Kamada, and Brandon
The Bad Boyz!
I love you Guyz

Story One
Crawl

It started on my chest. Small red and sore bumps. I could not explain why they appeared, but I knew deep in my heart I would not live to see them leave.

My chest ached and my breasts burned with an annoying itching that made me scratch until the bumps opened or may be they erupted on their own. This terrible itching continued for weeks, but finally eased only to move within both of my armpits. Now the agony truly had begun.

Beneath my blood red swollen arms was a painful rash that drove me mad. I had to cut my nails to prevent myself from tearing the flesh from my armpits. With time my armpits slowly began to feel better, but then the itching moved down my sides and beneath my left breast and upper rib cage and also my poor neck.

But then the itching moved back under my arms. The pain, the burning, and the swelling filled my armpits with a horrible crawling sensation. I was beginning to realize and accept all at the same time that I was not going to get better.

I did not see a doctor because I did not care to. I never liked or trusted someone who was paid to pretend to care for or cure a person they did not know.

I tried to care for and cure myself, which I was not able to do. I became obsessed with the thought of waking up and going to bed itching and burning. But even worse than the driving, itching, burning pain that I had to endure was the insatiable urge growing in my mind: the urge to slither out of my skin.

For me time did not heal my wounds. Days, weeks, and months went by, but my condition only became worse. I had trouble sleeping comfortably due to my swollen neck and painful armpits. I hated how I felt and I especially hated how I was beginning to smell. How shall I put it? Like decay.

One night as I tossed and turned in my sleep I felt my armpits began to leak. As I slowly rose from my uncomfortable bed to turn on the light I knew without a doubt that it was not sweat pouring from my badly festering armpits, but blood.

I stared weakly into my bedroom mirror at my inflamed and rash filled body and watched my nightshirt soak up my infected blood. I realized that I had not cried once since the process of my decomposition began. That night I wanted to cry, but by then I could not because the rash had invaded my eyes.

I sat in-between worlds, the world of the dying and the world of the dead. My mind tried desperately to think of when and how I could have acquired the condition that was killing me. Was it the increase in my water intake? Was it the new vitamins I had been taking? Or was it the plant that had grown through the cracked window I could not close of the house I had bought only two months before?

I really did not know. All I did know was that I was moments away from leaving the terrible pain that had become me and I it behind. I was not afraid. I wanted to be released from the grip of agony. I wanted it all to end. I wanted to die.

When I opened my eyes again the pain was gone. I was free. No more itching. No more burning searing pain. No more bloody, painful, swollen armpits.

When I looked down at the floor I quickly knew why. The rash lay in a bumpy, bloody heap. The rash was Formless, but not lifeless. I had finally succeeded in slithering out of my skin. I watched in horror as it had the audacity to crawl away.

Story Two:
Pay Me Back

I bought this house around a week ago. I thought it was so beautiful, so comfortable. I should have noticed one thing about it though. The cold. The cold was an immobilizing chill that permeated my bones. I thought that once the boiler was turned on it would warm up, but it did little to ease the frosty nip in the air. The strange thing was that it was the beginning of October. And what was even stranger was the fact that no one I invited to the house could feel the cold.

The only warm place in the house was my bedroom. It was a very large, but dark room that left me feeling warm, yet not comfortable. My bedroom was the only room I could stand to be in due to the freezing atmosphere throughout the house. There was something else about the house that made be feel a bit unnerved other than the cold. The consistent throaty request made by my unseen occupant. "Pay Me Back!"

I heard the male voice the second night I moved into the house. I was in the kitchen preparing a sandwich, which was to be my dinner when I heard the eerie chant that sounded even more chilling than the cold.

I called the police and they searched the entire house, but did not hear or find anyone. At least while they were in the house I felt safe and secure. After they left I knew I was not alone. Not only did the eerie male voice start his pleading song again, he began to show himself limb by limb.

First, his arms, then his legs, and then he stepped completely out of the shadowy hall and into my world. Entering the light did little to make him appear clearly to me.

His tall and masculine figure was barely distinct in the bright kitchen light. The dark image was surrounded by a cold mist of air that seemed to be emanating from his very being. He was the reason for the cold. The dark image opened its mouth and said, " Pay me back!"

My heart almost stopped. Here before me stood a man that was not a living man. No man, woman or child could live without a measure of heat throughout their bodies. I began to tremble and sweat even in what felt like the dead of winter. I can honestly say I was more than just a little spooked. I was scared stiff.

As I stood shaking from head to toe the dark image began to move slowly towards me. The closer he came to me the more I realized that the reason why I could not see him clearly was because he was clad in black. I could not run. I could barely breathe. The nearer he came to me the colder I felt. The dark image reached out his icy gloved hands and took mines into his. He held my hands with a strong grip and would not let go.

I struggled and with all the courage I could muster up asked in a horrified voice, "What do you want?" The dark image looked down into my eyes, his eyes as black as death and said, "Pay me back!"

"For what?" I asked in a bewildered voice. "Pay me back for the warmth I have given you." What was he talking about? What warmth? Did this dead man have me confused with someone else that he once knew? I was completely confused and scared.

"Don't you remember me Seche? It was a long time ago. A long time ago when you made me cold." I was beginning to remember who the dark image was. I was beginning to remember his kindness, love, and warmth. Warmth I could never return. Even though I wanted to so much I could not because I did not love him.

"I tried so hard to love you more and more each day, but you turned my love away. All I wanted was to keep you safe and warm. How do you live without the love of the person you love? You don't. You don't live Seche. I could not live."

I knew that he was right. You cannot live without the love you want. I also knew that it was my fault my new house was so cold. It was also my fault that Peter could never give or feel warmth again.

"I decided that if I could not receive your love I would never love again. I searched so long for you Seche and now I have found you." I wanted to cry, but my tears were frozen in my eyes. I wanted to shake free my hands, but they too were frozen. Frozen in his dead hands forever.

"I ...I didn't love you Peter. No matter how hard you tried to make me I just didn't love you." He looked into my eyes again with his dark blank eyes and in a hideous enraged voice said, "Didn't? No Seche you couldn't love me. You can't love anyone, but yourself. You never even tried. Even in the bedroom you pretended to love me. Because of you I learned to hate bedrooms. It became a place of lies. I found that I could not enter them without thinking of you and what you took from me. But tonight I did not come here to make you love me. I came here to get back what you took from me. Pay me back Seche. Give me back my warmth."

I felt a strange feeling taking over my body. The cold I felt upon my flesh was becoming a part of me like the air I breathed. It took less than a minute, but for that minute a thousand regrets passed through my soul and filled me with sorrow the like of which I had never felt before.

I watched the back of him as he walked slowly towards the kitchen door. Taking with him the only trace of warmth I would ever feel again.   And the house and I remained cold.

Story Three:
Night Of The Witch

I was around 10 years old when it happened. It was a dark and silent night, as I lay in bed sick with an upper respiratory infection. As I withered feverish and in pain, trapped in a land between the restless and the resting, I felt a strange thing happen.

Something small and dark was at the foot of my bed. Afraid, I did not dare raise my head and look in its direction. I just lay there still awake, still asleep.

I felt the small dark thing began to climb onto my bed as I lay motionless able to move, but daring not too. I sensed that this small dark thing was not human. It was something terrible, something bad.

My pain grew worse as my bed began to soak up the sweat that was seeping from my young pores. I felt the monster move with slow calculated movement onto my bed and then onto me.

Just as I felt its small yet heavy body upon my body, I sprang up into bed and knocked the vile thing off of me. It proceeded to jump off of my bed and without looking back, wobbled towards the hallway that led to the kitchen.

My heart was racing no longer out of fear, but out of excitement. I was not scared. I needed to know what had tried to do God only knows what to me. I jumped out of bed and made my way quickly down the hall and into the kitchen.

I stood in the kitchen watching the wind blowing through the cracked window. The crack was big enough for something dark and small to climb in and out. The weird thing was this, my mother always kept the kitchen window closed and locked.

I never found out what the dark small thing was. That was the last night my family and me stayed in the small apartment in The Bronx. The next day was moving day. We moved into a large old house that always felt cold. But only two years after moving into the house my parents sold it. My family could no longer live in the house with all of its strange happenings. It was like every room contained some sort of evil vibe. Almost twenty-five years later, I bought the house back.

I have been living in the house only five months and a lot of creepy things have happened to me, but like the night the dark small creature tried to get me, I feel no fear.

My family is astonished that I have bought the house again and my family to this day will give me a mystified look whenever I tell them the story of the small witch. What they do not understand is that if I am ever to find out what the witch wanted with me it will be in this house.

I believe that some place in this house the witch waits for me. The last night in the apartment in the Bronx I returned to bed, fell asleep, and dreamed after the dark small thing I call a witch disappeared. In the dream I saw myself searching throughout this house for the witch. And when I found her one of us screamed a frightening scream. I have to know if the scream came from the witch or me.

The house is hiding and protecting her. In one of these rooms I will relive the night of the witch and then and only then will I be able to leave this house. Well, that's what the house promised me anyway.

Story Four
Ghoul

Heath Stevens had been the way he was for as long as he could remember. He was tall, dark, handsome, and morbid. Heath lived in a world filled with gloom and sadness. Life meant nothing to him, but death, death meant everything.

Not a day or night would go by without Heath thinking or dreaming about the world in which he did not have to worry about the troubles that life brings. Heath thought and dreamed of the world of the dead.

Heath Stevens lived alone in a house that seemed to accept and adhere to his desire for all things dead and buried. The house was his confidant and his refuge from the living. Without the house he had lived in a little over five years, Heath knew without a doubt that living would be even more unbearable.

Although Heath was thirty-six, he never knew the love of a woman. This bothered him sometimes especially during the evening when feelings of aloofness proved to be too much to live with, but death would not come.

Sometimes he dreamed of the perfect woman who would share his desire to be freed from the living. Heath Stevens dreamed of a woman who wanted to die with him. He dreamed of a woman who wanted to kill him and he her.

In his twisted mind Heath saw himself clad in a brand new navy blue suit, white shirt, and black shiny shoes. Heath saw himself with his dream woman who was dressed all in white dancing to music the house played, the sounds of souls moaning from every room in the house. They danced to the unchained cries of poor desperate souls who could never leave their unpleasant dwelling.

The house, with every turn and move, would show the lovers the world in which they both desired to go. A world filled with sleep and silence. But the whimpering sounds of the dying woman he kept locked in one of the upstairs rooms removed him from his solemn daydream.

The woman's cries had stopped, but Heath Stevens did not check to see if the woman had finally died after the long week in the hell he kept her in after she turned out not to be the perfect woman who shared his dream. The woman wanted to live. She told him he was a sick ghoul. She wanted to leave the house, but it would not let her go. The woman wanted life, so she deserved to live forever in the house.

Heath left the house even though he regretted leaving. But it was time once again to try to find her, the perfect woman who wanted to die with him. As He walked down the walkway the house stared down at him, smiling and hiding all the women who were not perfect for Heath Stevens.

Story Five:
The Epitaph

Rosemary Delanie
Born December 3rd 1968
Died March 12th 2003

Rosemary Delanie was a sweet young lady.
She was gentle, kind, and pure.
Never married, but self-assured.
She worked hard day and night.
And never stopped until she got it right.

Success was hers even when times for others were hard.
She built a life that was wholesome and good.
And never strayed away from her path.
Until the day she bought a house filled with an evil past.

Rosemary was alone in the house.
Lying casually upon her couch.
When she discovered the doorway that led to hell.
Once she entered she would not live to tell.

She should not have let her curiosity get the best of her.
She should have paid more attention to the bad things that
happened all around her.

Like the time her mother came to visit and suddenly fell ill.
Or the time her best friend Jude fell from the top of the
stairs and almost got killed.

But the house did not want Rosemary's mother or best friend.
The house only wanted her soul to bend.

The house wanted to turn Rosemary's good heart inside out.
It wanted to corrupt and deter her until she lost clout.

Rosemary Delanie where do you live now?
Is it within the rooms and walls of this house?
Where are your hopes and where are your dreams?
Can you tell me your secrets can you share them with me?

Can you tell me on that cold last night what you did see?

I see you in my nightmares are you warning me to get out?

I live here now.
Yes I bought your house.
I feel you all around me in the dark and in the light.
The house is stealing me as it stole you that night.
Please tell me what to do.
I have tried talking to you, but you will not speak to me.
That is why I was force to commit this obscene deed.
I have written this message that hovers above your grave.
My Epitaph for you Rosemary Delanie.

Story Six:
What Happened To Clara

The entire house was dark, save for the bathroom, which was lit with candles that sat on the closed toilet seat and window ceil. Clara, lay screaming inwardly as she pushed harder, breathed, and pushed even harder. She felt it coming. She felt it emerging from her sore and bloated body as she laid sweat drenched and weakened in the tub.

Clara prayed that the already fading candles would stay lit long enough for her to deliver the thing that had grown inside her for so long. But just as she felt the burning tear as it began to enter the world the candle on the toilet seat flickered then went out. The only light now came from the fast fading candle that sat alone on her window ceil.

Clara screamed. The force of its departure sent waves of nausea and pain throughout her entire body. Then the windows ceil candle dimmed and gently faded away leaving the bathroom in complete darkness.

Clara reached down between her soaked legs and felt for it, but she could not feel it. All she felt was warm blood. Her blood.

No Father. No pregnancy of which tests could find. No recollection of the day or night it was conceived. Just memories. She only had memories of anger, bitterness, and hatred.

It had vanished simply as if it had never been. But it was alive somewhere in the house. It was alive somewhere in one or may be all of the rooms. Clara's evil was somewhere alive.

And when the house had finished tormenting her and finally turned the lights back on she would have to find and face it alone, unprotected, and unprepared.

Clara heard a small voice say, "The world is my father. My father. The world raped and impregnated you, my mother. Let the world be judged for what it has done."

Clara felt her anger begin to subside, her hatred die, and her bitterness dissolve. Her heart and soul felt light as her burdened spirit removed the weight it carried for so long. But time and the house promised to give her a new child and once again its father's name will be man.

Story Seven:
Felix

"Stop calling me, stop calling me. Please stop calling me!" Felix, filled with exasperation and anger quickly slammed down the phone.

Felix was 24 years old and lived alone. He thought himself lucky or in better words, blessed to have his own business and home at such an early age. It was not often when a person his age could be so successful and admired. But he knew he had worked hard to get where he was.

Felix owned a small computer gaming corporation and spent many hours creating, co-creating, and approving the latest action and horror games on the market. But none of the games he created could compare to the terror he was experiencing with his ex-girl friend Sheila.

At first, everything seemed normal. They went to the movies, shows, plays, and romantic dinners and their love life was very exciting and sensual. But soon after they had been dating. Felix noticed a change in Sheila's behavior.

First, Sheila would grab his hand and squeeze it tightly whenever another woman would look his way. Then it became even more intolerable. She would squeeze his hand and then pull him closer to her if anyone seemed to be staring at or getting too close to him. Felix suggested that maybe people were staring because of how attractive she was. But when things began to get out of hand like grabbing his private parts and arguing day and night about how he was cheating on her, he more than suggested that people were staring at them because of the way she treated him in public. This only fueled her jealous rage.

Sheila began to follow Felix wherever he would go. She would watch him and then finally accuse him of plotting against her with another woman.

Felix tried everything possible to make Sheila feel secure in their relationship, but nothing secured her heart that he was not going to leave her. After one night of violence that left Felix with a gash across his chest that required thirteen stitches, he decided that was exactly what he needed to do. He needed to leave her.

But, he did not, not right away anyway. Felix convinced himself that the knife incident was an accident caused by something he himself must have said or done. Although that something he just could not figure out for the world of him. Things were about to change and not for the better.

Felix stared hard at the lights in the roof of the ambulance as he tried desperately to figure out how once again he had allowed himself to be beaten down by a petite woman. A woman he thought loved him. But his thoughts began to fade as he lost consciousness due to the blow Sheila had given him with the handle of her umbrella.

After spending two days in the hospital for a mild concussion, Felix decided that enough was enough. Sheila Courtney had to go.

At first, Felix felt proud of himself. He felt more relaxed and confident. More like he used to before Sheila. Felix felt sure he had made the right decision. He was glad he let Sheila go. But he still could not make his love for her die.

Two months had passed since he had seen or heard from Sheila. Life was right again and things were fine until Felix met another woman.

Sheila was there. She was always there. When he picked up his new girlfriend Dianya. When they went out to dinner.

When they went for long walks. Felix could see her beautiful, yet scary eyes watching them with hatred and jealousy.

That is when the phone calls began. Sheila would call Felix just to breathe at first. Then she started to tell him things. Horrid things. "I love you Felix. Don't think that I don't. Even if I hurt you again remember it's only because I love you so much! Remember that whatever I do it's because I love you."

Felix was upset by her phone calls at first, but then his confusion and sadness gave way to frustration and anger. He did not go to the police because he still loved her and did not want to cause her trouble. Besides, Sheila did not need help from the law. She needed deeper help than that.

Felix, felt sure he had made the right decision in breaking it off with yet another girlfriend. He did not want to involve Dianya in his troubled life. And although she was bewildered by his unexpected and abrupt decision, Dianya sadly accepted it. Just one more quality Dianya had that Sheila did not, Felix thought sadly to himself.

It was a dark rainy and uncomfortable night as Felix sat alone thinking of a way to resolve his problem with Sheila when suddenly he heard a noise. No, it was not just a noise, but footsteps.

The lights went out. It was the fuse box. He had to check the fuse box. Felix bumped his left knee as he stumbled in the darkness trying to find the entertainment center where he always kept his flashlight handy.

The flashlight gave out reasonable light, but Felix could not wait to have all the lights back on again. He almost dropped the flashlight when he heard the sound of small running feet. Then he heard her call his name.

Felix's flashlight hand kept shaking as his heart started beating rapidly. She was in his house. Sheila was in his house. "I still love you Felix. Now why you want to go and cheat on me ha? Didn't you know that I'd know if you tried anything nasty like that? But I know you still love me because you got rid of that man-stealing bitch. Lucky for her you did it when you did. Because I had something special planned for miss clean-up."

Felix almost threw up thinking about how Sheila must have been in the house whenever he and Dianya were alone. Sheila had been watching and hating them the entire time.

"Sheila, honey where are you? Come out where I can see you. Let me turn the lights back on so we can talk okay?"

Felix bit down on his lip in anticipation of her reply. But all he heard was silence. The silence was much worse than hearing her say no.

"Sheila, baby can you hear me? Answer me please." Then he heard her laugh, a small chuckle to be exact. It was a chuckle he had always despised. It sounded to him as if she was secretly laughing about some bad thought she was having about him. He was beginning to wonder why he still loved her.

"Kiss me Felix. Come find me and kiss me the way you used to before you threw me away."

Felix could not control his tears. He felt weak like a child. His voice broke as he spoke, "I...I didn't throw you away hone, I simply told you that I didn't feel that we should be together anymore. I still care for you. I always will, I think, but you have to stop doing this. Now come out where I can see you."

A minute or two passed before Felix heard her run up the stairs. Slowly he made his way towards the stairs.

"Kiss me Felix, I'm waiting for you. Come kiss me and love me again."

Felix walked slowly down the hall and as his hand continued to tremble he dropped the flashlight. He bent down and felt for it. But finding it did no good. Some how it stopped working. As horrified as he was he could not believe what he was thinking to himself, "$25.00 down the drain."

"I...uh, where are you Sheila? Tell me where you are." Sheila chuckled again. "I'm in here you fool. I'm in our bedroom. Come and kiss me."

Finally, Felix found his bedroom door and turned the knob. The room was pitch black and very cold. He heard Sheila chuckle and followed the hideous sound over to the bed.

As he lay upon the bed it too was icy, but not as chilling as the small petite hands that caressed his body. "Kiss me Felix. Kiss me and love me." Felix was shaking, not just from the cold, but also from his repulsion for Sheila and the madness that had consumed her.

Felix, lay upon Sheila's cold body and kissed her frozen lips. The entire time he thought to himself, "Tomorrow, I'll get Sheila the help she needs."

When Felix opened his eyes it was morning. It was a whole new day. By Felix's side lay nothing. His bed felt warm again and his naked body, it too felt warm. He felt lazy and dreamy as if he wanted to lie in bed forever. But he could not. He had to help Sheila. He still loved her after all. He truly understood this now. He loved her and always would.

Hours had passed since Felix had tried calling Sheila, but could not get a response. Fearing the worse, he realized that he had to call the police.

As he explained the entire story to the detective word for word, he felt a heavy burden being lifted off his shoulders. He realized that he too needed help. Felix needed absolution.

"Son..." the detective calmly said as he place his hand gently on Felix's shoulder. "Ms. Courtney couldn't be the woman you've been seeing and she most certainly couldn't have been in your home last night." The detective paused as Felix stared down at his hand still supportively on his shoulder. "Ms. Courtney is dead. She passed on over two months ago. Don't you remember son? You both were in an automobile accident. You suffered a concussion and some minor cuts and bruises. But Ms. Courtney died from massive head injuries."

Felix continued to stare wildly at the hand that was on his shoulder. He then spoke in a shrill voice. "No...no, no. I know about the car accident and I know all about her dying. Don't you get it? She's not dead, not really, not in the sense that we think we understand death. She's here. She won't let me go. She won't let me love."

"Mr. Landers, please calm down." Felix sprang up from his chair. "No, I won't calm the fuck down. You think I'm seeing things don't you? You think I'm all mixed up and confused and that I'm so broken hearted over her death. But I'm not. I still love her, but I was glad when she died. I was free. Well, I thought I was free. But she's not gone. She never left. I don't know how it's possible, but I'm telling you that girl is still alive some where in my house."

Felix left the police station inwardly enraged, but he pretended to be calm in order not to get locked up. But he knew he was right and some how he was going to help Sheila. She had to understand that their relationship was over. Love had nothing to do with violence and Sheila was too damn violent, even in death.

Felix's phone rang. It continued to ring until he picked it up. Silence. Then he heard her voice. "I enjoyed you last night Felix. I'll be coming over real soon. Don't cheat on me. Remember I love you Felix."

The phone went dead. Felix stood with the receiver in his hand for a moment then casually sat back down on his black leather living room sofa.

"No one understands. It doesn't matter that she's dead. She's never going to leave me."

Felix sat back, closed his eyes, and listened. He waited to hear the sound of her petite footsteps. He waited to hear her annoying chuckle and he waited to feel her icy touch. He waited because deep in his heart he knew that he would always love and need her. The house knew this too.

Some Dreams Do Come True. Even If They Are Bad!

Story Eight:
The Drummer

When I was eight years old he came for me, as I lay upon my bed arousing from my morning nap. I got up early that spring morning too early to go to school. So I decided to lie back down and get a few more minutes of sleep.

Suddenly I felt my inner eyes open, as my physical eyes remained closed. I sensed that I was not alone. My dream eyes slowly looked up and hovering above me was the most horrifying sight my mind could visualize.

His face was large and malevolent. His body was short and stout. He appeared to be strong and bold. His face and entire body seemed to shimmer as he played his death March song. A song I knew he only wanted to play for me.

He played, as I lay there motionless without a word. I listened to the rhythm of his song. Brump, brump, bru...mp. That is what it sounded like to me.

He looked down at me with an intense serious glare. One that let me know that he was truly there.

The death March song was carefully played. He never missed a beat. I was sure it could be heard throughout my family's new house. A house I hated and wanted to leave.

The drummer vanished, but left me with a feeling of unease. A feeling that told me that some day once again we would meet and he would play his song for me one last time.

Story Nine:
One Night Stand

To Belinda Oxford the man seated next to her at the bar appeared to be just the type she wanted to take home with her that night. He was tall, dark and handsome. But most of all he looked like an easy target. Someone she did not have to worry about getting attached to. He was perfect for what she had planned.

Belinda was smooth. She did not wait for him to notice her. She made the first move. Belinda offered him a drink, which he gladly accepted with a smile. She noticed how beautiful and bright his smile was. He had full lips, kissable lips. But that was not the only thing she noticed about him. Belinda noticed his eyes. They where the deepest brown beautiful eyes she had ever seen, yet they were completely empty.

It did not take long to spark up a conversation with the stranger. He was kind and gentle and had impeccable manners. They talked for almost twenty minutes before they both decided to leave. The only problem was Belinda, used to getting her way, wanted the stranger to come home with her, but he wanted her to come home with him instead.

Finally, Belinda decided to take a chance and go to his place. After all, she lived with her roommate in an apartment she hated. And here was a man who lived all alone in his own house.

As he was driving her to his home Belinda began to reconsider her decision. But it was too late. Before she could change her mind he was already pulling up the driveway.

As Belinda stared at the house a creepy feeling began to fill her body with dread. Her blood began to run cold. But the stranger gently took her hand and smiled his full beautiful smile as he stared at her intensely with his empty eyes.

Heath Stevens led the woman he prayed would be his dream woman into his house. There he hoped to convince her to love him to death.

Inside his house he would dance with her. Alone in the house he would caress and hold her until the flesh fell from their decomposing bodies.

Oh how he wanted her to be the one. But she was not his dream woman. He knew it in his heart the moment she entered the house and found the woman who only hours before had aroused him with her pathetic whimpering from his dream world.

Belinda Oxford screamed in horror at the pitiful woman who appeared to have been starved to death. She ran towards the front door, but the house held it shut. She pulled out handfuls of her long black braids as Heath Stevens looked at her in disgust.

Heath ordered her to stop screaming as he held his hands over his ears. He could not stand to hear the sound of a woman crying. Heath began to laugh hysterically trying to block out her screams. Then he began to chase her through the house after she ran away from him like a mad woman running away from a straight jacket.

"Don't cry. Why are you crying?" Heath asked her as he held her tightly in his arms. "Don't worry I'll take care of you and give you what you want. If you want to live forever you have come to the right place. Here you'll stay in the house where you can flirt your life away."

Heath teased Belinda all night long. Trying to dance with her to the houses song. But no matter what he whispered in her ears she still wanted to live.

Heath could not understand why anyone would want to live forever when death was so sweet and so comforting. All he wanted was someone to die with, but he knew he would not find her tonight. He was so tired, so very, very tired of searching.

Belinda Oxford felt drained as she rested against Heath's chest. She thought back to the bar and how she should have never tried to play Heath. Heath obviously was a player who had been playing a deadly game with his own set of sick rules for a long, long time.

Heath continued to kiss and chuckle in Belinda's ear, as he explained why he could not let her leave. The house promised to let Heath rest with his dream woman if and only if he could find her. And the ones who ended up not being the one for him the house would keep forever alive, forever alive in the house.

Belinda allowed herself to be led upstairs to a darkroom where she knew in her heart she would never leave again. And for once in Belinda Oxfords life she wished she had spent one night without a one-night stand.

Story Ten:
All Three Of Nando's Ladies

Nando Wallace pressed against the cab's backseat door as he solemnly watched the people, stores, and buildings slowly disappear as he left the city behind. He disliked the one-hour ride that took him to Ms. Maxwell's creepy old house. As a matter of fact, he disliked Ms. Maxwell too.

Nando was only fifteen, but he was tall for his age. Maybe that was the reason why his mother treated him as if he were already grown up. His mother Toshina and her busy body sister Nora were the ones who made him come to work for Ms. Maxwell everyday after school even on Saturdays. "We need the money!" They both yelled at him. "You're old enough now to help make ends meet." His mother made sure to remind him everyday that it was his fault she had to give up her dreams of becoming a famous painter. Her paintings were alright, but he doubt very highly whether or not she would have been famous even if she had not let his father impregnate and abandon her.

It did not matter anyway. They were always broke, so they needed the extra money. And in his aunt Nora's words, "If you want a place to stay you'd better work boy."

But he did work. He worked hard from 4:15PM to 9:00PM cleaning, cooking, and getting yelled at by Ms. Maxwell. Ms. Maxwell was a divorced woman in her mid forties who blamed the world for all her so-called misfortunes. She had money, but that was all she had. She never had visitors. No family or friends. At least none that Nando had ever seen or heard of. All Ms. Maxwell had was money and her creepy old house.

When the cab pulled up to the driveway Nando's heart sank. There she was waiting for him with a look of intense anger on her twisted face. He wondered what he had done wrong this time in her eyes.

"Now, tell me for the thousandth time why you're late again Nando. I mean, don't you understand that when you promise to do something be it fixing something or arriving on time you should keep that promise?" Nando looked at his watch. It was 4:21PM. He was six minutes late. Rather than argue with her, Nando simply nodded his head in agreement and mumbled a half-hearted apology as he walked passed the angry petite woman.

It was 6:45:PM when it happened. As Nando was preparing creamed chicken soup for her dinner, Ms. Maxwell came rushing into the kitchen waving a large, black old book yelling something about not touching her things.

Nando stood with his back to the stove watching the enraged little woman as she continued yelling and waving the book at him with tears in her eyes. "She's insane." Nando thought to himself. But before he could apologize for having touched her book, she slapped him.

Rage filled Nando's heart as he touched the left side of his face feeling the sting of her slap beginning to settle in. It was not the first time he had felt a woman's hand across his face. But it would be the last.

Nando grabbed the large, black old book from Ms. Maxwell's small hands. With one mighty blow he silenced her tongue. At that moment he heard the house say, "Good boy. And now the others Nando."

Nando Wallace, Pressed against the cab's backseat door as he cheerfully watched the people, stores, and buildings slowly reappear as he left the house behind. He enjoyed the one-hour ride that took him to his mother and aunt's cramped little hole in the wall. As a matter of fact, he was going to enjoy the one-hour ride back. After all, the house was going to have two new occupants. The house promised to take care of all three of Nando's ladies.

Story Eleven:
Evil Bones

In life all I ever wanted was a house a place to call my home.
But no home was I to ever buy; yet in death I would build my
own.
Before my eyes closed for the very last time, I visualized
every brick and every stone.
I built my house with bodies of those who were the blame.
Their blood I used to paint my house a gruesome color red.
It complimented my solemn mood that of the dead.

Once I closed my eyes and fell into my eternal sleep it did not
last long.
For when I opened them up again the house and I were
joined.
I gave my life so that the house could live and live it has
done.
My walls are filled with human residue and the floors are
filled too.
If you do not believe me come inside and I will prove it to
you.
I have beaten and mangled those who dared to enter my
abode.
I have stripped them down and made them reveal to me their
bare souls.

So enter if you dare my place of fear and witness firsthand.

How a person drained of hope and love can die and return in
despair.
I died with a name, but no one cared, so I will not either.
I have cursed this house inside out, every brick, stone, and
fiber.

The rooms are dark and the house is cold just so you know.
There is one room waiting for you in which you will reveal to
me your woes.
But by then it will be too late you will have seen my evil
bones.

The End

About Horror

I have always written horror stories too many to count. There is something in the word horror that seems to bring out the best in me. Strange is it not?

The word horror to me means dismay, but also means experiencing and facing your worse fears. If you are strong and believe in God there is no evil no matter how horrifying that can touch you.

The characters in this book all had to face horror in the form of a house. Some survived their fears by accepting the inevitable. Like the child in story eight entitled *The Drummer*.

But most of the characters in the book submitted to their fears and allowed the house to corrupt and use them. In story four entitled *Ghoul*, Heath Stevens allowed the house to turn him into an insane monster that preyed on women with the hopes of finding death in the arms of a dream woman who shared his morbid fascination with death.

Horror is real. It lives, it breathes, and it is all around us. But if we face our fears and allow our goodness to fight against the horrors in our lives, we can move far away from the *fright houses* we build within ourselves.

About Me

My name is L. Roberson and everyday of my life I fight against my fears. I try with God's help to live in a world filled with horrors. I have built many Fright Houses and have managed to move out of most of them but...

I still live in some of the houses. One day soon I pray that I will be able to move out of all of my Fright Houses.

Evil Has No Boundaries

~~~The Evil Walls~~~

By L. Roberson

*This book is dedicated to my babies Karon,
Kamada, and Brandon
I will love you forever
Auntie P*

Part One

/No One Believes Me /

Chapter One

No one believes me when I say that wherever I go there is a presence in the walls. But it is not just in the walls it is also beneath the floors and on the ceilings. I cannot explain it any better than this: This presence hates me, spites me and wants to drive me insane.

I know that this presence is real because I have felt, heard and seen it. This presence is driven to do evil things to me. So now I realize that I must do something to protect myself before it is too late.

You see I have learned a long time ago how to play the game. It is quite amusing how the tables turned once I learned how to deal with the presence in the walls, ceiling and floors.

Sometimes it does not matter to me at all when the presence begins its task of driving me crazy. I simply go about my business and ignore it. Sooner or later the presence dies down. Why? Because it knows that it cannot affect me so it falls dormant, at least for a while.

But sometimes, only rarely, I become angered by this presence and this is when I become vengeful. I retaliate and give the presence my own form of punishment. *I curse it.* It then becomes despondent and confused.

But the game is much more fun. For example, whenever I take a bath the evil goes crazy. All I can hear is banging, hellish banging against the walls. The noise is meant to disturb the cleansing process. The presence continues its sick torment, but I began to play the game and the game is called *SILENCE.*

Quickly I turn the water on just enough to bathe then silently begin the cleansing process. The presence becomes confused. I can hear and sense it listening and waiting for a sign that I am there suffering on the other side, above, or below. But I never give myself away and the presence is forced to play along else it will give its own self away.

The presence is trying desperately to force its way into my home. It follows me from room to room. It is always present. It is trying to make me do something horrible. It wants me to kill.

I am a bad person, but I am not the worse person on earth. I am capable of doing horrid things. I believe this with my heart. But I also know that I will not allow the bad in me to be enticed by the presence to commit murder. Yet I will kill. I will kill the evil presence that haunts my walls, ceilings, floors, and myself. I will kill it and be free.

By the way, there is another presence that has already managed to invade my home. The filthy, smelly, dark thing suddenly and unrepentantly slipped its way into my home bringing with it an aura so black and vile I feel repulsed just thinking about it.

Day after day, night after night and moment by moment I am tormented to the point of madness. My breath being breathed, my footsteps being followed, and my thoughts are corrupted. Yet, I do not fear either presence. I am not afraid, but enraged. I have a feeling that the echoing footsteps of my predators are about to cease.

Noise and certain smells have always had the power to affect my mind in negative ways. Loud obnoxious sounds such as music turned up to the maximum, talking as if one is trying to tell the world his or her business, banging against walls and slamming doors also makes me crazy. Some how the presences that torment me found this out and are using it against me in an effort to destroy me. Why? I know its secret. I know what it is and it does not want me to tell. But I will tell. I am telling its secret now.

Chapter Two

The presence in the walls, ceilings, and floors is suffocating me with its annoying mockery. I cannot breath without taking in a breath of anger. I am surrounded by hate. The hatred the presence feels for me and I for it. And as for the presence inside my home the overwhelming dread and gut wrenching detest I feel cannot be explained in words. What I feel can only be felt and no one can feel my feelings, but me.

When I fall asleep my hatred stays awake inside of me. There is no peace living with this emotion building inside me. It will erupt one day and when it does the hatred will flow from me like waters freed by a broken dam.

You should know that the presence entered my life around four years ago. I lived with my family in a small rundown apartment on the first floor after we lost our house. The small cramped dump turned out to be a hellhole not fit for decent human or animal life. But we endured the flooding, the rats, the insects, the garbage and the yearly rent increases by our slumlord.

As I struggled to live in these unhealthy conditions I began to hear the presence creeping around above my head. The presence was barely audible, yet I could feel the cruel and building evil intent in its footsteps.

I tried to tell my family about the presence, but they claimed not to hear the footsteps coming from above. After all, the apartment above was empty. I knew that this was not true. Something was living not in the apartment, but within the ceiling itself.

Now, I know this does not make sense to those who have not experienced the presence like I have, but it is true, all of it.

Soon after I discovered the presence I began having extremely violent thoughts. Sick thoughts. These thoughts were about killing people who wanted to spite my family or myself. Who were these people? These people would be anyone who decided to live in the apartment above us. I believed that whoever moved in this apartment the presents would take them over and they would try to destroy us.

And like I suspected when a family finally moved in above us things became unbearably worse. The family above acted normal at first, but then the presence in the ceiling, which was their floor, began to control them. That is when the stomping, banging, dragging sounds started.

When I would see the family coming or going they were always polite, yet once they entered their apartment all hell would break loose. I am not talking about the normal sound of footsteps, but the sound of something with hooves.

As the months went by I could not tolerate the abuse any longer, so I took matters into my own hands. I began to torment my tormenters.

I sabotaged their lives by threatening them and causing them to live in constant fear. I recall once threatening to cut them up into little pieces and if finally, after months of mental torture they had not moved I would have cut them up.

Once again the apartment above us was empty, but the presence only became more forceful. But a few months past and my mother decided that we would live in the apartment above and of course I did not like the idea not one bit. But eventually we all agreed and moved into the apartment above where the presence lived in the ceiling.

But now the presence was in the floors, this only proved my theory that the presence did not live in the apartment itself, but within the ceiling, which was now our floors.

Chapter Three

I could hear the constant sound of hooves on the actual floors as well as claws scraping on the ceiling of our old apartment. Through it all no one believed me even though I knew in my heart that sometimes my family could hear it too.

How strange life is if we live long enough to think about it. We are born into this mysterious place called the world, yet we do not live long enough even if we live past a hundred, to explore and figure it out. I had to know what was living in the ceiling and floors above and below me. But before I could discover what it was we moved. After one year living downstairs and three living upstairs my family and me were out of there.

Do not get me wrong, I was glad when we moved. Actually we have only been living in our new home for a little less than four months. Now the presence has followed me and it resides not only in the ceilings and floors, but also within the walls.

The presence is very dominant and strong now that it has found its way inside the walls. But I am stronger and even more dominant. I know that soon, very soon I will face this evil presence and make it bow down to me.

Am I depressed? Am I hysterical? Am I apprehensive? Am I exasperated? Yes, yes, yes, yes. Well, let me not go completely crazy, at least not yet.

Guess what? There is no sound coming from the ceilings, floors or walls. I suppose I should be grateful, but I am not. I could give a sweet damn that the presence believes it is affording me this rare moment of peace. I will not be fooled. It has plans. Believe me it is working on something big and it intends to attack when I will least expect it. But I know it. I know it is feeding off of my faults. It wants to devour me alive, but I will not make it easy. I am not as delicate and tasty as I look.

I never lose faith in the way I feel or what I believe no matter what others may think. I know if I do not kill this fiend it will kill me.

No blood flows from the ceilings, no blood pools the floors, and no blood runs down the walls, yet I can see death permeating these places.

Death is the end of our journey. Death is the beginning of our release. Death is at the center of our fears. The presence that lives in the ceilings, floors, and walls have traveled through life and experienced the ecstasy of letting go and it takes sadistic pleasure in our qualms.

My fears are being brought to the surface, the prospect of dying has left me empty and from these I can find no respite. Because of the evil presence these things have made me realize the truth. I will not be amongst the fortunate ones who live their dreams, but the unfortunate ones who must fight to survive their worse nightmares.

My long brown hair is turning gray even though I am only in my late thirties. I feel old beyond my years. My body hurts as well as my soul. I have allowed the evil presence to evolve as I deteriorate. My heart is broken, but I will not be broken. Soon the presence will go away forever. I must make sure that when it does I remain behind in my entirety.

Why did this have to happen? Why do I have to do this? I must do it because I have no choice. The evil presence has left me with no choice. I have to kill it. It must die if I am to be saved.

I can smell the rotten stench rising in the air. It is preparing to torment me. It is 5:01 PM. It is almost time for my nightly bath. I want to kill it now, but tonight is not the night. It is not time.

Part Two

/The Will To Kill/

Chapter Four

Stop and rewind. Let us talk about the game. My game. It is the game of *Silence*. The *Silence* game is not like a regular game. It is an amusing little pastime, a very intensive diversion.

I play the game very well I think. But like all games the players will learn all the rules and learn how to play. The evil presence will learn the rules and how to play, but before this happens I will change the game.

The human *will* can either be very strong or very weak. Individuals who possess a weak *will* are unable to do things especially bad things. But individuals who possess a strong *will* are able to do very wicked things. My *WILL* is very strong!

I *will* conquer the evil presence that is trying to destroy me. I *will* not wait for it to invade my life like the one that presently exists within my home. I *will* rip open the ceiling and dig up the floors, and tear down the evil walls.

When the ceiling begins to shed tears and the floor becomes a salty pool all the walls skin will bubble up and ooze away baring the evil presence's soul.

My apartment is very cold now and my family will be going away for a while to visit relatives. I will be alone here with the evil presence. I am not afraid, but "*It*" is. While my family is away I will remove the evil from my home. I am ready. I always have been. My *will* is stronger than ever.

/The Dream /

Chapter Five

This morning I had a dream and in this dream beige walls surrounded me. I was trapped inside my apartment with no furniture and no family or so I believed.

I became enraged as I stood in the beige maze and started banging on the walls. I began to scream something along the lines of "I hate you!" And/or "I am not afraid of you!" I could sense the evil presence silently listening to my angry words while it relished in my anguish. This angered me even more.

Eventually I ran out of my room and to my mother's room, but her door was gone. In its place was a beige wall. I began to bang on the wall as I was screaming that something was trying to destroy me. Suddenly, I could hear my mother's almost inaudible voice coming from behind the wall. She was telling me in an exasperated tone that I knew there was nothing in the walls. Her voice sounded small and cold. Perhaps it was not even my mother. I could feel her presence as well as that of one of my younger sisters behind the wall, but they were very weak. I believe that the evil presence was probably trying to trick me into believing they were both trying to harm me. It wanted me to lose trust in my mother and sister. No matter, it was working. I was angered beyond reason with them both.

Then it happened. After I went back to my room I heard loud banging music coming from the ceiling. The music grew louder and louder as I lay in bed staring at the ceiling ranting and raving words I cannot recall.

No one else claimed to hear the music or the banging. But just the same whatever was in the apartment with me was not my mother or sister.

I Am So Angry!

I woke up alone and angry. I could not differentiate between the walls in my dreams or the walls I was now staring at. Yet the rage I was certain of. It was real. It came straight out of my dream.

/Health Issues/

Chapter Six

I am sick and weak. My head hurts most of the time and my entire body feels as if I have been frozen alive and slowly thawed in a twisted effort to cause me as much pain as possible. My muscles and bones are killing me. I know in my heart I am not well.

This is one of the main reasons why I need to defeat the evil presence in the ceilings, floors, and walls. It is killing me. I know that it is. I can feel it. But another thing I have begun to realize is this; If I get rid of the evil presence that has some how managed to enter my home the other evil will dissipate also.

My throat hurts. I have been yelling inside again. The evil presence can hear me when I yell inside. No one else can hear me though. Perhaps my family can see my screams inside my eyes. Perhaps they can see two small versions of myself imprisoned by the evil presence. My family, I am trying to escape and finally be free.

/Living Will/

Chapter Seven

When I die everything I own will go to my babies (my three nephews.) Hopefully they will not have to endure the horrors I have over the past few years.

They will get it all. My babies will inherit my rare antiques, collectibles, books, music, and money. Do not be misled I am not rich, but I have managed to accumulate quite a few valuable objects in my lifetime. I hope they enjoy them. I sure as hell did not get the chance to.

I pray that they do not inherit the evil presence in the ceilings, floors, and walls. No, I will make sure that they do not.

My will be done.

Desecrations, Fantasies, and Superstitions

/The Desecration /

Chapter Eight

It was in the bathroom, but I did not enter. The foul smelly beast was waiting for me. The dirty, dark bastard was stalking me. I heard the spiteful bitch as it roamed about my room where I cleanse my body, mind, and soul. But I stayed put and finally it moved away form the bathroom. But my anger remained.

I visualized cutting my abdomen open a few minutes ago. I saw and felt the knife as I made a deep incision starting from the left and ending at the right. It felt good. I did not bleed much, but I could see the thick neatly cut flesh open and smiling up at me. At the time I did not know why I had this sadistic thought, but now I do. I was releasing the rage trapped inside of me. It helped, but only a little.

The ceilings, floors, and walls are still silent. I am still not fooled by the evil presences. I still feel like I am being watched and my world desecrated.

As The One

I Thought I knew you not long ago
I knew your laugh
I knew your cry
I knew your deepest desire
But I knew nothing about you
You sinful liar
The only truth I know resides in me
I know the truth and it will set me free
Your hidden dark secrets cannot hide from me
I have a light that helps me see
You have incapacitated me with your constant
taunting
You have left me stony and icy
But like a stone thrown
I will shatter your glass
And like ice I will put out the flames you burn me
with
I will know you again
Your laugh
Your cry
Your desire
I will know you again
As the one I Admired

By L. Roberson

"It is not the fear itself that makes us afraid, but the expectation of the fear itself."

-Lydia Roberson

Part Three

/Sleight Of Hand /

Chapter Nine

If I told you that there was a killer who tried to break into my home in order to kill me you would probably believe me right? If I could show you proof that a knife-wielding maniac had attacked me you would probably believe this also. Why? We all know death and violence is believable. We read about or sometimes witness the most horrific crimes mankind is capable of. Yet, I know that when I say that there is an evil presence trying to destroy me you probably do not believe me.

If our eyes can see it then it is real right? Wrong, not always. Sometimes what our eyes see is not always the truth. Our minds can fool us. Our minds are where we find meaning from what we have witnessed. But what if what we have witnessed is but a mere fantasy or a strange illusion? What if the fantasy or illusion is so real we believe it to be the truth? Would it matter? I mean if we truly believed that what we have seen is real would it change the affect it had on us? My answer is no. I believe that if we believe something is real then it is real.

Call it a *Sleight of Hand*. What is real and what is fantasy? Fantasy, make believe, or an illusion, it does not matter because if we believe our fantasies etc. they will affect out lives in reality. So if the evil presence that surrounds me is but a mere delusion brought on by a fantasy it does not make any difference whatsoever. It has produced a very disturbing illusion that has affected my life in a terrible way. But the truth is the evil presence is not a fantasy or an illusion. It is real.

/Writing On The Walls /

Chapter Ten

When I was a small child my mother, grandmother, and older sister would tell me not to write on the walls. But of course I always did it any way. I would scribble my name and sometimes the little obscenities I picked up from home and school.

I knew at an early age that it was only a superstitious belief. I never believed in superstitions. I still do not believe in them, but I will say this; just because I do not believe in superstitions does not mean they are not real. Like I said earlier, "If we believe something is real then it is real." But I also believe that *if something is real it can affect your life even if you do not believe in it.*

Even though I do not believe in superstitions some how I find myself bringing the subject up. Maybe some how it was I who *drew* the evil presence into my life. Maybe I wrote some sort of invitation so many years ago that the evil presence finally decided to accept. May be it is possible that even though I do not believe in superstitions they believe in me.

Writings On The Walls

I wrote words upon the walls
My sister teased me and threatened to tell all
I tried to wash it away with soap and water
But that just made her tease me even harder
You cannot wash it away
She explained
The evidence of what you have written will still remain
There were some truths in her warnings
I washed away the writing
But I removed the paint
Now what was written there my parents would think
I cannot remember so long ago
Whether or not what I did was revealed
Or if I was punished for the silly messages scribbled about
nothing at all
But I may be suffering for the childish writings on the walls

By L. Roberson

/The Pipes /

Chapter Eleven

I finally understand how the evil presence entered my home. It came through the pipes. One morning as I was cleansing myself I heard it as it traveled through the pipes in the walls. It did not know I was in the process of cleansing myself because it was not my usual time of cleansing. I had decided to cleanse myself earlier than usual because I was not feeling well and I wanted to get my morning started. It is strange how I never noticed the evil traveling this way before.

It sickens me to know that I have drunk the evil waters that have passed through the pipes, which flows through the faucets. I have cleansed my body in the evil waters. The entire time I believed that I was cleansing myself when all the while I have been drawing the evil into my own body. How strange.

I have found another of the evil presences secrets. I know its passageway. Now I must find its entrance and block it.

The Passage

You know your way into my world
You travel quite often
Through pipes like blood through veins
Like the soul encased inside of body
Like skeleton inside flesh
You claim, but shall not remain

/The Obsession/

Chapter Twelve

Outside of myself I dwell sometimes beyond my home, yet always inside its realm. Never ending and always near. It is an invasion, but not within. Surrounded by my own insecurities and fears, yet I am not afraid only angry.

I admit that I am quite mad, but who would not be given the same circumstances? I am tired and weak. I am sad and hopeless. I am suffering beyond reason. I cannot feel or think of anything else. I am alone and my mind is obsessed. This has gone on long enough. It must end soon. It must end now.

/The Heartbeat Inside Cold Walls /

Chapter Thirteen

Last night I was awakened by a terrifying sound. It was the sound of muffled hoarse laughter. As I crept out my bed and over to the wall from which the sound was coming from I placed my ear against it. I trembled for a moment. The wall felt like ice.

The laughter died down and was replaced with sad cries. The sound was heartbreaking and tears begin to well up in my eyes as suddenly something happened. I realized to my horror that the sad cries were coming from me.

For the first time in months I had become frightened, not of the evil presence, but of myself. It was beginning to dawn on me. Was some part of me living inside the ceilings, floors, and walls? But what scared me most was the idea that I myself may be a part of the evil presence that haunts me.

Lick

I can feel the cold breath that you inhale and exhale
I can feel the hot blood that flows from your veins
I can smell the degenerate flesh that covers your bones
I smile then lick the wall in order to taste your soul

By L. Roberson

/Alone With The Shadows /

Chapter Fourteen

At night I sleep blessedly and mostly do not awaken. Yet my sleep is not filled with peace I still find myself able to creep. Through my closed lids I see beige top to bottom wall to wall and that is not all. I can smell the rot of the evil struggling to break free and live. I am not a fool I am on to you, you sick, sick brute.

You think you are smarter than me. You think you will claim my soul. But I will hang fans from your ceilings and pictures on your walls. I will dance the night away pounding my feet on your floors.

Will you still be able to see me? Will you still be able to torment me when alone I stand in the shadows to face you presence to presence?

I am coming!

I AM COMING!

/Voices Moving/

Chapter Fifteen

Get out! Get out! Bear with me as I expel the evil. The time is now. It has begun. I can hear it, the laughter and cries. Oh God I can feel the sorrow and pain. Let it be over with. Stop it God. Remove this evil from my life.

The voices are traveling from wall to wall and my ceilings are roaring obscenities. The floors are freezing my bones. The evil presence is trying to kill me.

I see you. I can see you now. You are Black and horrid. Your skin is like old leather and your breath is like death. I hear you laughing, but I am not crying. I do not fear you. I am not afraid.

The invading presence is slouched before me now. I can see it clearly. It has something to say. Spittle is falling from its putrid black mouth.

"I waited a long time to come for you. You think that I am foul and unworthy of your presence. You see me as no one else can. I am the foul thing you feel I am. I do not deny this to your face. I will remain with you like a growth remains with its victim. I will infest your body, mind and spirit with my clotting black fluid. I will never allow you to

be at ease. *Your suffering is the reason for my existence. I will follow you to the end of your lifetime.*"

Its eyes are closed and its skin is dripping oily sweat. I hate it. But it has given me the last bit of knowledge I need to expel it from my life. *"Your suffering is the reason for my existence."* I know its entrance point. I did indeed let it into my life.

You taught me to isolate myself.
You taught me never to trust.
You taught me to imprison myself.
You Taught Me To HATE!

It was not the writing on the walls or anything else I could have said or done. But it was I who allowed you to do this to me. I gave you the power to make me turn inwards.

/Breaking Down The Walls /

Chapter Sixteen

The evil presence in the ceilings, floors, and walls is not evil. I am not evil. But I am trapped. I have followed myself and tormented my mind for many years now without ever really knowing the truth. But now I do. I am the presence I believed was evil for so long. The laughter, cries, banging, screaming all of it me. It was myself trying to escape the true evil. The evil seed planted inside my head by the *"Thing"* that helped my mother bring me into this world.

It is inside my head from above and below
It is all around me
The negative view of the world
The only world I will ever have or know
So much time gone
How sad, how terribly, terribly sad
The world is filled with bad, but it is also filled with good
I have been deceived
I have been tricked
And now my mind is trapped inside the ceilings, floors, and
walls
And this is the sad truth about a horrible lie

By L. Roberson

The Touch Of Fear

Step into the shoes of fear. Climb inside its clothes. Stand tall and walk away taking with you only one thing more; the understanding that where you leave it, it can never find you and you will be free to flow.

As you go on your journey towards the place where your fear came to be allow yourself to cry or laugh even though you might still be afraid. Your fear will not stand in your way unless you give into its habitual ways.

Climb the hill or enter the closet wherever your fear belongs. Release it now because it is time that you moved on. As you walk away leaving your fear behind it is safe to look back. Remember its face and its lust, but most of all never ever forget its hindering touch.

Fright House Morals

The characters in Fright House all have a shared quality. They all looked forward to something bad happening to them and it did. For example,

In *Crawl* the woman anticipates that her skin will not heal and it does not. She gives into her fear and allows her own skin to steal her life.

In *Pay Me Back* Seche anticipated the cold way in which she unintentionally treated Peter would ultimately consume her and it did.

In *Night of The Witch* a woman anticipated that eventually "Some thing" she called a witch would return to claim her body the way it tried to one night when she was a child.

In *Ghoul* Heath Stevens anticipated the prospect of life. For Heath being alive was a death sentence. He never learned to appreciate or adjust to the world in which he had no choice, but to live. Heath Stevens did not have the courage to end his own life, so he preyed on women with the hopes of finding his death mate who would do the job for him.

In *Epitaph* a woman anticipates the same fate as Rosemary Delanie. Rosemary was a woman who allowed her fears to consume her.

In *What Happened To Clara,* Clara gives birth to her anger and sets it free. Clara anticipates being impregnated and giving birth to her anger once more.

In *Felix,* Felix anticipates spending the rest of his life devoted to a woman who he both hates and loves even in death.

In *Drummer* a woman anticipates her death after hearing her funeral song years before in a vision as an unearthly being plays it.

In *One Night Stand* Belinda Oxford anticipates her death after foolishly accepting an invitation to Heath Stevens house. A man obsessed with the idea of finding his perfect death mate.

In *All Three Of Nando's Ladies* Nando anticipates a life of abuse by the hands of the women in his life, so with help from the house he becomes a killer.

In *Evil Bones* a dead woman's hatred and fears still live inside the house she built. She anticipates the worse in those who decide to live in her house and that's exactly what she gets.

You have just examined the morals of the stories inside Fright House. Now, write a short poem or story based on one of your own fears. After you have done this read it to yourself and search for the moral of your poem or story. Focus on the lesson it has to offer and learned from it.

Don't anticipate or give into your fears.

www.ingramcontent.com/pod-product-compliance
Lightning Source LLC
Chambersburg PA
CBHW031859170626
46807CB00004B/1799